For my mother, who raised my spirits every Halloween.

For my husband, who never questions my spookiness.

For Jim, Clara, and Emi, may you enjoy every Halloween together as much as I do!

— The Halloween Queen

All Hallows' Eve Press
806 Main Street
Poughkeepsie, NY 12538
www.allhallowsevepress.com

Ordering Information:

Quantity sales. Special discounts are available on quantity purchases by corporations, associations, and others. For details, contact the publisher at the address above.
Orders by U.S. trade bookstores and wholesalers. Please contact All Hallows' Eve Press:
Tel: (914) 489-9529; or visit www.allhallowsevepress.com.

Printed in the United States of America

First Edition

Library of Congress Control Number: 2011916318

ISBN-13: 978-0615534190 (All Hallows' Eve Press)

Illustrations by Rob Peters
Illustrations © 2011 by Donna Davies
Text © 2011 by Donna Davies
Book design and production by Rob Peters, www.rob-peters.com
Editor: Miranda Paul

the Halloween Queen who lost her Scream

An EVIL Blue Fairy Tale

By Donna Davies

Illustrated by Rob Peters

In deep, thick woods hides a secret town,
Where Halloween monsters seldom frown,
And Calliope rules as the Halloween Queen—

She sulked in her room with tears in her eyes.
"Who stole my scream?" she wondered, "...and why?"
The Queen tried and tried but just couldn't scream.
"Oh no! Now there will be...NO HALLOWEEN!"

The Halloween monsters went batty with the news.

The black-widow, Mina, said
she'd look for clues.
"Calliope and I are like peaches
and cream;
I'll find out who stole her
Halloween scream."

Calliope freed Mina, and set her back down.
Then Mina pointed out blue glitter on her crown.
"Helene! Helene!" shouted the furious Queen,
"That evil blue fairy swiped
my Halloween scream!"

The Queen pleaded to Mina, "I need a cure, now!"
Mina wanted to help, but didn't know how—
Then in roared the Screamin' Demons
fast on their bikes.
Mina got an idea! "Warren— time for a hike!"

"Don't worry, my Queen! Meet me at the clock tower,
I'll find you a cure before the witching hour!"
Mina hopped on a bike and away they zoomed,

To find Witchy Wanda with
her spells and her broom.

Mina spied Zak creeping out of the trees.
She knew he could help, and told him to "FREEZE!"
Then she explained, "We need wet zombie drool–"

Zak spit in a tube
and thought it was
cool.

They passed by The Lab on Mad Scientist Court,
Home of Frankenstein's monster (Frankie for short).
"Snake!" Warren screamed, then started to squeal,
"How perfect," yelled Mina, "Cause we need an eel!"

But would they find a 200-year-old vampire?
What luck! There came Vlad, dressed in vintage attire.

Vlad knew he was needed,
the word got around,
So he proudly donated the best
blood in town!

Sam was **SHAKING** a skeleton dance.
He was so entertaining they
watched in a trance.

Then wind howled through twisted trees in a gust.
The watchers awoke— and grabbed Sam's bone dust.

At the cemetery they met Crypt-keeper Clyde.
Standing inside rusty gates that spanned twelve feet wide.
Clyde looked at the list, "You need this for the potion!"
And he peeled cherry bark to show his devotion.

"What's next?" said Mina. "Oh no! Blue fairy glitter."
Warren spotted Helene. "Let's reach out and get her!"

Mina SPRANG into action,
tying silky threads tight.
Helene flapped like a kite—
Oh, what a sight!

"We've got everything," said Warren, quite pleased.
They whizzed back to Wanda's through the dark trees.

They put the ingredients in her
cauldron and stirred.
Wanda yelled, "One more thing
and the Queen will be cured!"

Mina sneered at Helene, "Give up
the glitter, Fairy!"
"Never!" said Helene, "You're not
really that scary!"
Witchy Wanda yanked the silk
as hard as she could,
The blue fairy glitter fell into
the pot where it should.

Warren rushed the potion back into town.

Queen Calliope, who was waiting,
drank it all down.

Every monster was there–except for Helene!
Quickly, however, she was spotted by the Queen.

"I'm sorry," Helene said,
"I wanted a part in Halloween.
We all know blue fairies are
CURSED, to be mean."

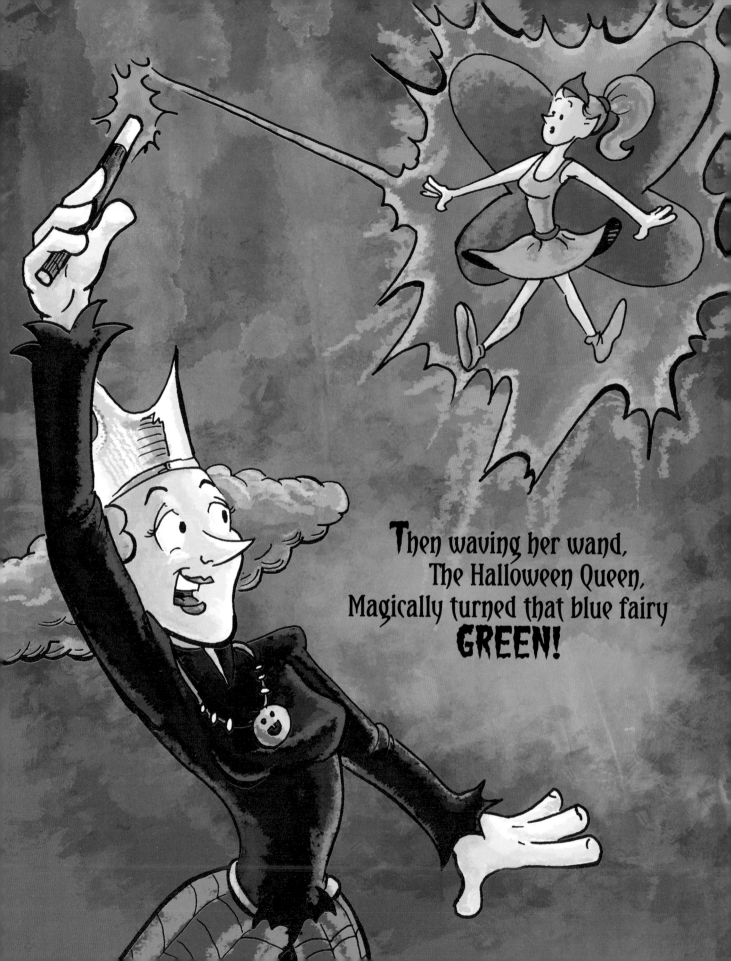

Then waving her wand,
The Halloween Queen,
Magically turned that blue fairy
GREEN!

She chanted, "I forgive you Helene my dear, Halloween will always be the best time of the year!"

Made in the USA
Charleston, SC
25 June 2013